Acknowledgements

My thanks to Lorraine, who edited my manuscript into

a readable script.

INDEX

ILLUSTRATIONS

Chapter 1

SURPRISE IN THE GARDEN

"Grandad, there are pixies and fairies in the pond."

He looked down at Charlotte with such understanding, realising she was so young.

"Well my dear, why don't you tell me all about these pixies and fairies?" he said with a smile.

"I saw two boats in the pond, one with fairies and the other with pixies in it," Charlotte said, with Matthew her brother agreeing.

"I saw them as well, they sailed in a tiny boat with a sail made of an oak leaf." Grandad looked at both of his favourite grandchildren (as he only had the two) and said, "I think the only thing to do is have a good look, don't you?"

Charlotte and Matthew took Grandad's hand and pulled the unconvinced grandfather towards the pond, hurriedly pulling him quicker and quicker towards the waterfall. As they got closer there was a strange smell in the air, a warm, gentle, intoxicating aroma. Grandad could feel something was different as they came closer to the water. The children squealed with delight as they arrived at the pond.

"There I told you!" Charlotte said in an excited tone.

To the astonishment of Grandad, there were two tiny sailing boats in middle of the pond. Their oak leaf sails bellowing in the gentle wind as both boats glided between the lilies. On each boat sat a pixie and a fairy, sitting under a daisy umbrella and all seemed very peaceful until a scream from one of the boats rang out.

"The humans are watching!" a voice shouted.

This was terrible, as fairies and pixies were supposed to be invisible in the daytime.

"Our invisible dust must be running out," Apple Blossom said, in her gentle Cornish fairy voice. Flautles, the pixie, held Apple Blossom's hand and said, "Don't worry my dear, we will sail to the other side of the pond and disappear into the undergrowth."

Grandad, Charlotte and Matthew looked in disbelief as the tiny boats steered towards the pebbles on the other side of the pond. They watched as four tiny figures jumped out of their boats, and ran through the garden disappearing out of view.

"Do you believe me now?" Charlotte said, looking up to an astonished Grandfather.

"Yes, my dear, I do."

As the fairies and pixies disappeared, the smell also left. They all stood in total silence and disbelief as they watched the little boats gently rocking from side to side against the pebbles. Then a soft mist floated over the pond and waterfall leaving a strange feeling of mystery.

Chapter 2

DAVID THE GARDENER

David pushed his wheelbarrow to the flowerbed he had nearly finished weeding before the weekend. To his horror all his hard work was now covered in weeds.

"I don't believe it!" he shouted.

"It is as if they had been planted by someone, just to annoy me," he said to himself, as he took his tools out of the wheelbarrow.

It was a lovely warm morning with a slight wisp of wind blowing from the west, and the birds happily chirping in the trees. David sunk his fork into the soil and started weeding the patch again. Suddenly there was a strange sound. He looked up to where he thought he heard the noise. It sounded like laughter. David leaned on his fork and listened as hard as he could.

"There it is again," he said to himself, "I must be imagining it."

David spent a few more minutes listening and there it was, yet again. The sound was coming from behind the large clump of Michaelmas Daisies. David stood up and moved quietly closer and hid behind the statue. He suddenly saw a glimpse of something. Then blinked as a shape appeared, sitting on a toadstool. As he looked closer he could see a figure laughing to himself, with his little hat and bell bobbing up and down. Slowly the figure started to become clearer and David could see the shape of a small round figure.

"What are you?" David whispered, as he didn't want to frighten it.

"I am Billy Bucka the Cornish Piskey," the little Piskey said.

"That's an unusual name, what does it mean?"

"My name comes from an ancient Cornish myth which says that Merman are believed to come from the sea and live deep down in old mines."

Billy Bucka was only about four inches tall, but he looked very dapper in his pointed hat and matching yellow waistcoat. The buttons on the waistcoat shone brightly in the sunlight, and he wore trousers that went all the way down to his little pointed piskey shoes, and to finish his attire off there were two bells on the end of each shoe. David was amazed at what he saw. He leant down and said, "Do you have anything to do with all the weeds in the garden?"

"Well! I don't personally, but I know who does," Billy Bucka replied.

After a few minutes he had explained all about the Weed Gnomes, the Plant Pixies and everything else that happens in a garden after the sunset.

"How is it I can see you now, as I have heard laughter in the undergrowth but not been able to see you before?" David enquired.

"Well, unfortunately we all are running out of the invisible dust that keeps us from being seen. There is a problem in the mine and we can't get enough of the green stone needed to make our invisible dust."

David looked down at the little gnome and felt rather sorry for him.

"Maybe I could help you get some more stones," he said.

The little piskey looked at David and smiled. "Oh, that would be wonderful."

Suddenly, a haze came over the patch of soil where Billy Bucka sat and he disappeared. David stood in amazement as he poured himself a cup of ginger tea from his flask. He looked around and there was no sign of the creature. So, he turned around and went back to his laborious task of weeding again.

His next job was to mow the lawn, so he made his way to the shed and pulled on the old latch. The door creaked as it opened, and soon David had pulled out the lawn mower and pushed it across to the lawn to where he was going to start. As he pushed the machine across the grass, he soon noticed the mower kept stopping, so he looked at the blades and found they were jammed with wet grass. David found this most annoying as it was a hot sunny day and he quite expected the grass to be dry and easy to cut. On and on he pushed, but cursed, as the grass seemed to be getting wetter and wetter. Suddenly he stopped and heard a quiet giggle. He looked down and there was a sprinkle of water pouring from nowhere just above the lawn.

"This is why the mower keeps clogging up", David said to himself. The water kept coming from nowhere, and then suddenly a figure started to appear holding a watering can. David was amazed as he could see a little gnome watering the grass.

"What are you doing?" David quietly asked, trying not to frighten the little figure.

The little gnome looked up at the gardener and suddenly realised his invisibility had stopped working and he could be seen. "AH!" the gnome said with a gulp.

"Do you realise the problems you are causing me?" David said.

"Well yes, that is the whole point of me being here," The little gnome said with a slight smile and snigger. "My job today is to slow your mowing up as much as possible, so the humans will give you the sack."

David looked down at the little chap and smiled. "My dear little gnome, no matter what you attempt to do, you will never get me sacked as I am a friend of theirs."

The bemused gnome looked down in shame and put down his little watering can, "I am very sorry," the little gnome said as he turned around and walked slowly across the wet grass. His little bells ding-donged as he moved. His left foot was a ding and the right a dong. The merry sound filled the afternoon air, until eventually he disappeared behind the hollyhocks and the last quiet dong could be heard. David felt a little sad for the gnome, as he was only doing his job, and then continued mowing a lovely dry lawn.

Chapter 3

AGRAN'S SHED

Agran, the Chief Weed Gnome, lifted one of the jars from the shelf and blew the dust from it. The label read *Old Dandelion Seeds*. He then placed the jar on the table and sat back in his rocking chair and waited, as he knew tonight was weed night. Soon there was knock on the door and he quietly shouted, "Come in."

The old oak door creaked open, as the weed team appeared, one by one they settled around the old table where Agran sat patiently waiting.

"Good evening Agran, may I just say what a pleasure it is to be here this evening."

Agran smiled and then shook the young elf's hand.

"Why thank you, young elf. I am so glad you could make it, as I know how busy you both are."

"Well, yes, we have had a rather busy day what with sharpening tools, cleaning pots and of course cleaning our shoes."

Agran looked down at their very shiny shoes and smiled. "My, aren't they clean."

"Oh thank you," Crabgrass said.

I would now like to introduce you to the Weed Team. At the head of the table is Agran, (Head of the Weed Team). On the left of the table sits Catnip and Mugwort, two young gnomes. On the right sit two young elves, Crabgrass & Ragweed.

"Now the seeds in this jar have been collected over many years, and are ready to be sown," Agran said.

Everyone leaned forward and peered closely at the dusty jar.

"It's a very dusty jar, Agran. How old do you suppose it is?" Mugwort asked.

"Well, I have been here 25 years and it was here before then, so it is quite old," he laughed.

"Now spring is nearly here, and we need to start the sowing," Agran said.

The Weed Team always loved this time of year as winter didn't produce many weeds, but spring on the other hand did, and made everything grow much faster, especially the weeds. Unfortunately spring was only two weeks away and everything needed to be sown as quickly as possible. "Now, I have a new invention," Agran chuckled as he pointed to a large contraption in the corner of his shed. The machine had a long barrel-shaped wheel at the bottom and a sieve above it, with a wooden frame holding it all together resting on four large metal wheels.

At this point, I think I should describe Agran. He is a portly gnome and very friendly, but he has a strange sound in his voice. When Agran speaks he always sticks his tongue out, and this makes him sound very odd.

"Agran, could you please demonstrate your voice for us?" Crabgrass asked with a snigger.

Agran stuck out his tongue and said, "Good evening my fellow Weed Team".

As you can hear he sounds very odd. But maybe you can't, as this is a book so it is impossible to hear him. Although, if you now stick out your tongue each time Agran speaks and say the words with him, you will understand what he sounds like... Let us now get on with the story.

Agran stuck out his tongue and said, "I would like to demonstrate my latest invention. Now, all you have to do is put the seeds in the top of this sieve and as the machine is pushed across the garden, they gently fall to the soil."

Everyone looked in awe at the marvellous wooden machine when Mugwort said, "What is it called?"

"The Weedoclapper," Agran answered.

He stood up and turned the motor on, and then climbed onto a chair. He then poured a few seeds into the top and jumped back down. Then he pushed the machine slowly across the shed as the seeds settled on the wooden floor.

"Well!" shouted Catnip.

"That's amazing," Ragweed laughed, as he got a dustpan and brush and swept up the precious seeds. They all clapped and applauded, and then started to laugh and titter at the thought of David's face after the Weedoclapper would have done its mischief.

Crabtree and Ragweed have also got another hobby. They paint the flowers with a special paint to make them the wrong colour. This is because they are Weed Gnomes who prefer weeds and they know it will confuse the gardener as he pulls them up by mistake when he doesn't realise they are flowers.

"When shall we start sowing?" shouted Catnip.

"Tonight, just after midnight," Agran laughed,

"As we need to get as many seeds sown before spring as possible."

As he said that, the church clock struck midnight, and everyone knew it was time to go.

The night air was still warm and hung over the garden as the gnomes pulled the Weedoclapper across the lawn towards Agran's potting shed. Once inside, Agran put a selection of acorn shells on the table, "I think we should celebrate," Agran smiled, as he poured some elder wine into the acorn shells.

They all stood up and lifted their drinks.

"To a weed filled spring!" Agran said to his fellow chums.

The gnomes repeated, "To a weed filled spring.

Chapter 4

THE INAUGURATION

"Well, it's that time again,"Agran said, as he stood behind the altar and waited for the proceedings to start. The inauguration ceremony has been held for many years but no one can remember when it originally started.

Agran first was reputed to have started the Gnome Weeders many, many years ago, and is now buried by the side of the old mine under a large granite stone. All the gnomes and elves waited in anticipation for the ceremony to start as they surrounded the altar. The gnome's parents had brought their young Gnomerettes along for them to be inaugurated.

"I will start with the Gnome Prayer," Agran said.

For all those days of toil and grind,
Let the gardener's life be cursed.
With all the weed s that he can find
Let's make sure they all grow first.

This was a very important time for the Weed Gnomes and their siblings as the old tradition had to be kept alive. The local band were always invited to play and, under the directorship of Normando, they played gentle weed music such as:

The Buttercup Prelude
Dandelions on Parade
The Clover Waltz

The Gnomerettes paraded very excitedly in front of the altar as they all waited for the ceremony to begin. As the music stopped, Agran said, "It is now my privilege to introduce the next generation of Weed Gnomes."

The Gnomerettes' ears pricked up as they waited in anticipation.

"It is time for the Gnomerettes to step forward and take their vows."

Quickly, the stage filled up with eager little Gnomerettes. They jostled and pushed to make sure they were noticed, as this was a very prestigious event.

"I would now like you to say the Gnomerettes' vow," Agran said.

One by one they stood up and prepared to say their vows:

I do swear to annoy and pester,
The gardener who tries his best here,
My job is to give him pain and grief,
While I employ all kinds of mischief

The ceremony continued with much elder champagne and merriment and the band played late into the night. Eventually, the old mine fell silent as the Gnomes and Gnomerettes went to bed. The two Naughty Elves, Crabgrass and Ragweed, who had maybe enjoyed themselves a little too much, were quite merry. On their way home they daubed everything in their path with their little brushes, leaving the garden covered in very jolly colours.

Chapter 5

APPLE BLOSSOM & FLAUTLES

Apple Blossom is the only daughter of Agran. She doesn't approve of what her father does during the evenings around the garden. She also loves Flautles the pixie. They both want to get married but Apple Blossom's father disapproves. He thinks Flautles is a waste of space as he is so timid, a bit of a silly sausage, and only wants to play his flute. Agran can often be heard mumbling about Flautles. "The only way I would ever let him marry my daughter is when he proves he is a proper pixie."

Apple Blossom and Flautles sat under the willow tree and watched as the gnomes started their evening's work. Their various machines were pulled around the garden by the white mice. Some machines were too big for just one, so several were hitched together with ivy vines for ropes.

"Apple Blossom, I have a confession," Flautles said.

"What is that my dear?" she said with a soft tone.

"Well..." he crossed his little legs and nervously fiddled with his flute.

"You know the lovely flute you bought me for my birthday?" he said with an expression of trepidation, "Well, it seems it will not work so well now."

"Why what has happened?" she said with the same soft quiet voice. Flautles looked coyly in her eyes and quietly whispered, "I think I might have left it in the rain, and it may be my fault that it isn't working quite as well as it should."

Apple Blossom looked crossly at Flautles, "Oh dear Flautles, I only bought you that flute last year, and you have ruined it already!"

Flautles sighed to himself. He knew he was a silly sausage but just couldn't seem to get anything right, no matter how he tried. Apple Blossom looked at Flautles with her soft gentle gaze, and sighed. "My dear Flautles what is wrong with you? You are always making mistakes," she said with a tear in her eye. "I understand you are a little slow and maybe lacking a tool in the tool box, but I do still love you so much."

Flautles looked deep into the eyes of Apple Blossom and could feel her love.

"Don't worry my dear, I will always forgive your mistakes," she said as she held out her hand and closed her soft fingers on his little hand.

"Thank you, you are so kind to me," Flautles said, looking longingly into her blue eyes. They sat for a moment and composed themselves, then thought about the gnome problem.

"What can we do to stop all the weeds being sown like this?" Apple Blossom asked as she held Flautles' hand.

They sat for a few minutes, when an idea popped into Flautles' head, "Why don't we find someone to make a magic goo that will kill the weeds?"

"I know, there is a Fairy Godmother in Lostwithiel who makes potions. Why don't we ask her to help?" Apple Blossom suggested.

They both thought this would be a marvellous idea and the next morning went into the little town of Lostwithiel where Jude, the Fairy Godmother, lived in a little shop at the bottom of the town. They both made their way to the shop and knocked on the little red door.

"Come in," the soft voice said.

Apple Blossom and Flautles both pushed the heavy door open and stepped into a cosy, inviting little room. There were huge cabinets filled with diamonds and pearls, with a big pile of teddy bears in the corner of the room next to a roaring log fire. In the middle of the room stood a huge table covered in all sorts of jars and bottles and, sat behind a large wooden desk, was Jude the Fairy Godmother. "Hello my little dears," she said in her distinctive Cornish voice. "Can I help you?"

Apple Blossom and Flautles looked up at the huge desk.

"Why don't you both fly up onto the desk?" the kind voice said.

They both fluttered their wings and flew up onto the desk and were soon sitting next to the vase of lilies.

"We were wondering if you might be able to make a magic goo to kill the nasty weeds in our garden?" Flautles said. The tremble in his voice was obvious, and Jude the Fairy Godmother said, "Please don't be frightened of me, I won't harm you."

They both looked up at her and smiled. Jude found a piece of paper and a pencil and started to write notes as Flautles explained what was happening in their garden.

"Leave it with me, I will come up with something to help," Jude said with a smile. Apple Blossom and Flautles were so grateful; they both thanked Jude the Fairy Godmother and flew down to the floor again.

"Goodbye," they both said, as they left the strange little shop and went home to their garden at Trewether Farm.

Apple Blossom and Flautles gently glided to a landing spot next to the waterfall, their favourite part of the garden, as there were plenty of places to sit in the shade. They sat under the Handkerchief Tree and thought how peaceful it was, as they looked at the trickling water bouncing off the pebbles. Flautles took Apple Blossom's hand and turned towards her.

"Do you know how sad I feel, knowing your father's resistance to us ever being together?"

Apple Blossom looked sadly at the water.
"It is so hard to explain how I feel," she sighed.

Flautles suddenly stood up.

"There might be a solution to the problem." Apple Blossom smiled.

"What is that?" Flautles wondered.

"Well, as you know, my father thinks you a bit too weak and doesn't think you are enough of a pixie to look after me," she said gently, not wanting to embarrass him. "And, as you know, the green gems are becoming harder to get since the Troll and the Grindles have been asking for additional slaves to get them out of the mine. And I have heard my father grumbling to himself about you having to prove yourself."

Flautles looked across to Apple Blossom. "What do think I should do?" he wondered.

"I know! Deep down somewhere in you is a brave, strong pixie, and all you need to do is prove to my father that you are."

Flautles thought for a moment and said, "Ahhh! There lies the problem. I am a weak, soft pixie."

Apple Blossom held his hand, "I will be by your side to keep you safe," she said.

The sun was starting to set, as the birds quietly went to sleep. There were soft fragrances floating across the garden, as the young couple sat on the grass and leant back against the tree trunk. They didn't need to say anything, as a strong feeling of love was enough to keep them entertained. Apple Blossom squeezed Flautles' hand.

"I have an idea," she whispered. "Why don't you go into the mine and confront the Troll?"

Flautles suddenly sat up and looked straight into her face. "Do you know how terrifying the Troll is, and the two Grindles are even worse?" he said, with a terrified quiver in his voice.

Apple Blossom took Flautles' hand in hers and smiled kindly.

"My dear Flautles, I love you so much and I know you love me, but the only way my father will ever let us marry is when you do something dangerous and brave."

Flautles had a deep worried frown as he gazed at the glistening water, then he turned to Apple Blossom.

"I can't imagine how my life will be without you with me," he explained, as a tear trickled down his cheek. "So I will do my best to confront the Troll," he said very seriously.

Apple Blossom leant across to Flautles and gave him a kiss on his cheek.

"Thank you, I knew you could be brave enough."

Chapter 6

THE SLAVE IS SELECTED

It was always a dreadful day when the slave had to be selected. The gnomes and pixies always gathered at the gravelled area in front of the mine. There was a strong sense of trepidation as this was the day the Troll picked its latest slave.

"Don't be frightened," Flautles bravely said to Apple Blossom, as he held her hand. There were many other couples doing the same and trying to comfort each other.

"This must be stopped," Agran said to his wife, as he put his arm around her to try and stop her crying.

"Oh no! Here it comes,"

The crowd groaned as the door of the mine slowly creaked open. Suddenly the Grindles appeared. They were two huge monstrous creatures crouching either side of the Troll. Their long thin bodies reminded them of a dog at the front but then looked like a snake with a forked tail at the rear. Their nostrils bellowed green bile and cruel red eyes looked like they could melt through steel.

The Troll stood about nine feet high with matted orange hair covering its body. Four black claws protruded from its hoof-like feet and both front hooves only had three claws.

"It's time!" The Troll screamed.

Everyone knew what that meant, as this was when the Troll demanded a new, young, strong slave in return for more green gems. The crowd realised these were essential to maintain their invisibility and had to accept the Troll's demands.

"One year this will stop," shouted a distant voice, not wanting to be seen.

The Grindles quickly turned and looked fiercely over to where the sound came from. Slowly they prowled over to the edge of the pit, where stood a meek, frightened little pixie.

"Give it a fright!" shouted the Troll.

The crowd watched in horror as the little pixie was grabbed by the ugliest Grindle and thrown across the gravel.

"Please stop!" Apple Blossom shouted. "He is only small and you are so big."

The Grindles turned their attention to the little fairy and in a flash both Grindles were glaring down at Apple Blossom and Flautles.

"Did you say something, insignificant fairy?" sneered the Grindle.

"She was only suggesting you might calm things down a little," smiled Flautles, as he stepped backwards and held on to Apple Blossom's hand a little tighter.

"Oh really!" the Grindle laughed. He sat back on his hind legs and thoughtfully said, "Hmmm, I suppose a little fairy like you can suggest to a huge horrible Grindle like me what to do! Can you?"

"Ah!" Apple Blossom and Flautles said in harmony.

"Oh no, we weren't suggesting you do anything of the kind, Mr Grindle, but thought you might like to consider again the strategy of what you are doing."

"Oh for goodness sake shut up you stupid things!" screamed the Troll.

"Yes, Troll boss. I think you're right," the Grindle said, slowly slinking back to the Troll's side.

"OK!" sneered the Troll. "I think we know the routine, you give me a slave and I will allow more green gems to be produced. Quite simple I would have thought."

The crowd looked around at each other, knowing what was to come next.

"I'm afraid it is time to select the annual slave," said Agran, as he stepped forward and moved to the middle of the gravel area.

"All young gnomes and pixies, step forward please."

There was a lot of slow shuffling as each youngster stepped forward. There were eventually ten unfortunate 'slaves to be' standing in a row in front of Agran. The Troll then stepped forward and slowly it inspected each one, looking at their teeth, muscles and ears.

"Why on earth does the Troll look at their ears, Flautles?" asked Apple Blossom.

"I think it is to see if they are big enough to take a good ear bashing."

"Really, that sounds very silly, don't you think?" Flautles replied.

"Not really," she answered, "because if they were too small, then they might not hear a very important order."

The Troll slowly examined the line of candidates and stood motionless in front of them. Then, slowly, it looked again at the frightened candidates, and the crowd gasped as it pointed its finger. As they glared at the extended finger, green and yellow smoke appeared from under its fingernails and a swirl of mist moved towards the quivering slave candidates and drifted to the biggest, strongest elf with the hugest ears.

"That's it! Decision made," shouted the Troll.

The Grindles looked up at their master and smiled. "Right, get it down into the mine straight away."

The Grindles grabbed the poor unfortunate gnome and clasped it in irons. Without mercy they pulled the crying slave towards the mine door. Everyone lowered their heads and sobbed as the Troll, Grindles and the slave disappeared through the old green door and out of view.

Chapter 7

THE WEED NURSERY

"Listen up!" Agran shouted. The quivering little Gnomerettes stood in a row. They had no idea what to expect. In front of them was a huge pile of fresh compost.

"I suggest you all take a keen interest in what I am about to say," Agran said, as he looked down at the trembling little Gnomerettes.

He was at heart a bully, but made out he cared for his little students. One little Gnomerette peed himself as he stood waiting. He tried not to show his embarrassment and slowly swished his shoe over the puddle with mud and smiled. Agran brought out a long white root, then produced a small pot with compost in it.

"As you see, I have in front of you a weed root and I will now show you how to reproduce this into a magnificent dandelion."

The Gnomerettes looked in awe as Agran placed the cutting into the pot and filled it to the top with compost. Then, after he watered it, he lifted the pot and said, "How easy is that? Now, as you see, we are standing next to a lovely pile of fresh compost."

The Gnomerettes gazed up at the huge pile of brown soil.

"Now that is done, the next job is to plant our weeds in the compost pile."

The Gnomerettes moved closer to the pile of compost, and leaned forward on their little metal spades and waited in anticipation for Agran's next instruction.

"As you can see, it is easy to plant any weed in this soft soil," Agran said.

"Is there any difference in the roots of a weed?" a young keen Gnomerette asked.

"Oh yes, here we have a long white root. This one is a dock. Here is a yellow splintery root, and this one is a nettle root."

"Come on, let's climb on top of the compost and start planting," Agran said.

The little Gnomerettes clambered up the steep pile of compost and one by one got to the top. It was very high for some of them, and one had to sit down to stop feeling giddy. Agran stood in front of them and demonstrated how to plant all the various weeds and then asked a small, interested Gnomerette to do the same. The little chap stepped forward with his spade and took hold of the long white dock root. He then made a deep hole in the compost.

"It will have to be deeper than that," Agran gently said.

The little Gnomerettes furiously dug further into the soft compost and then lowered the long white root down into the tapered hole; slowly he sprinkled some more compost around the root and firmed it in.

"Well done," Agran said.

The little Gnomerette smiled with relief and stepped back in line with the others.

"That is a good lesson done." Agran said, and pointed his wrinkly finger towards the bottom of the compost pile, as if to indicate to the Gnomerettes to climb down and go home.

"A good job done," Agran repeated to himself as the Gnomerettes disappeared into the distance, and Agran thought of the nice glass of elder beer waiting for him when he got home.

Chapter 8

THE ROBIN

Apple Blossom listened as the Robin sang his happy song.

"That is so lovely," Apple Blossom said, as she swung in her swing under the Apple tree. The robin looked down at Apple Blossom.

"It is a song I have just composed. I am rather glad you like it," he said with a chirp. "But you look so sad my dear. What is wrong?"

Apple Blossom sighed and said, "My father, Agran, won't let me see Flautles any more as he says he is useless and not a good enough pixie to marry me."

"Oh dear, that doesn't seem quite fair," Robin sighed.

"I have asked Flautles to confront the Troll, and he said he would but father isn't convinced he will."

Robin sat for a moment and pondered. He then flicked his wing and said, "The humans are now able to see all the gnomes, pixies, fairies and elves around the garden, as the magic dust is running out."

Apple Blossom had heard Robin talk about the mine problems so often she just let him continue rambling.

The Robin stopped chattering about the magic dust and suddenly sat erect on his branch and said, "I think a solution would be for Flautles to confront the Troll. That would impress father."

Apple Blossom agreed, knowing she had already asked him to do that task.

"And, as you know, robins are very clever at appearing from nowhere, so I will be able to help you look after Flautles."

"How can you do that?" Apple Blossom asked.

"Well, if you come into my body you'll be able to be near him as I fly into the mine with him."

"How can I get in your body?" she asked.

"Well, there is a potion my mother showed me once, that shrinks fairies."

"Yes, but how do I get inside you?"

"Simple, when you're small enough you can fly in through my ear," he laughed.

"Goodness me!" Apple Blossom said, "What a clever idea."

Robin smiled to himself, as he was never shy about taking a compliment.

"How will I know when it's time to fly in?" Apple Blossom asked.

"If you sing my latest song, I will know you are ready," he said.

Apple Blossom thought for a moment and then started to remember the robin's latest hit tune.

"*Dum de dum de dum de dum de dum de dum.*
How's that?" She asked.

"Perfect, my dear, I think we are ready to go. If you look under the large mushroom over there, you will find a small bottle." Apple Blossom flew over to the mushroom and found the bottle. On the label it said,

'Only drink one gulp.'

So she opened the little bottle and took a single gulp. All of a sudden everything around her got a lot bigger, and she realised she had shrunk. As Robin said that, two magpies flew across the garden.

"There, that is proof everything will be OK" Robin said with a confident smile.

"Now if you kiss the mushroom, you will return to your normal size."

Apple Blossom did what Robin said and instantly grew to her proper size.

"Well, I think we are ready for when it's time.

AGRAN'S STOREROOM

Agran's storeroom was very impressive. There were many machines, and each one had an important use. As you enter the double doors into the storeroom, there is the *Flying Pink Weeder* on the left. This was a very simple machine, which was constructed in the shape of a box. On the top was a seat covered by an umbrella. Lower down were the *Seed Throwers,* which consisted of sieves that turned as the machines moved forward. These constructions were built on four metal wheels and were pulled by four hefty white mice.

Next in line was the *Dandelion Driller.* This was similar to the *Flying Pink Weeder*, but had a drill shaped construction at the bottom. The operator would select the appropriate dandelion plantlet, and then lower the drill. This would drill out a very deep hole and, when deep enough, the operator would drop the dandelion into the hole. It was then filled with soil and watered.

A slightly more devious machine was the *Couch Grass Winder*. This was a particularly evil construction as it made the life of any gardener as hard as possible, especially David. The driver of this gadget would sit on his plush red seat and watch as the long lengths of couch grass were loaded. Then thin wire would be wound around each bunch of grass root, hopefully making it almost impossible to cut through with any gardener's spade.

Then there was the *Seed Blower,* a huge wooden fan with three legs acting as a tripod. In front of the fan was a large box into which fluffy seeds were placed. The fan was then positioned in the garden, overlooking a patch of soil. There was also a long belt attached to a handle and, as one of the weed gnomes turned the handle, the fan would blow the seeds all over the soil.

The largest machine sat proudly in the middle of the shed. There were six chairs on a circular platform where the Gnomes would sit and make the white dandelion seed heads. They would take a length of straw and paint it green, then glue a small ball of cotton on the end. They would then stitch tiny lengths of dandelion seedlings into the cotton, which would then be dropped into a hole in the middle of the machine and wait to be placed in the soil.

Chapter 10

THE BRAMBLE CREATOR

Agran sat at his desk reading *The Bramble Creator,* when the shed door flung open and in the entrance stood a large gnome with a huge fat tummy. He stood with his legs slightly apart, and his hands resting on his hips. As he spoke, his curly grey hair bounced over his large red ears.

"Good evening," the stranger said.

Agran looked in amazement at the size of the stranger's tummy.

"Can I help you?" Agran said.

"Yes! I have come to show you my latest invention," he boastfully blurted.

"My name is Brambles, or Bram for short or B to my friends. Of course to my very best friends I will answer to a pout of their lips."

Agran sat bewildered as he looked again at the article he had been reading. There was a picture of the new *Bramble Creator* and standing next to it was the same fat, arrogant gnome that now stood in front of him.

"Is this you?" Agran asked, as he turned the magazine around to show him.

"Of course, I invented *The Bramble Creator* and have come to sell you one."

Agran leant back in his large rocking chair and stroked his chin. "How much are you asking?"

Brambles leant forward and put his big fat red hands on the desk. "To you 100 didrams."

Agran thought for a second or two. "How about 60?" Agran said

"75 and it's yours." Brambles laughed.

"OK, I'll have it. When can it be delivered?" Agran asked.

"You don't have to wait, as I have one outside on my cart."

Agran stood up and they both went outside to the cart. Brambles pulled down the ramp and he slowly rolled the machine down to the dusty track.

"There, what do you think?" Brambles asked.
"Very impressive, I look forward to annoying David with it," Agran said, shaking Brambles' hand.

AGRAN SWAPS PLANT LABLES

After much thought and deliberation, Agran had devised a very clever way to annoy David and make sure his gardening was as delayed as possible. Agran's plan was to raid David's tool shed and swap jar labels. He and the other weed gang waited until David had put all his tools away for the day and watched as he got onto his old grey mare and went home. His shed was at the bottom of the lower garden, it was only small but held all the tools and sprays he needed. The gnomes made their way to the shed, confident they would not be disturbed. It was easy to get in, as he never locked the door.

"There! What do see before your very eyes?" Agran asked.

Catnip and Mugwort looked at the tools hanging majestically from their hooks. The large spades and forks were on the left, progressing round to the sheers and hand tools. On the shelves were jars and bottles of all descriptions.

Agran looked at his helpers and laughed. "It's time for work, we are now going to make David's life a little more difficult."

Crabgrass looked up at Agran and smiled. "What is the wicked plan you have in mind?" the excited elf asked.

"We are going to swap the labels, as I will show you." Agran held the jar and indicated with his long wrinkled finger. "As you see here, the label says weed spray but we will swap the label with nettle seed. David will then think he is spraying weed spray, but unfortunately will be sowing stinging nettles."

They all turned to each other and burst out laughing.

Unbeknown to the gnomes and elves, Apple Blossom and Flautles were watching what was going on through the broken pain of glass under the honeysuckle bush.

"We must stop this," Apple Blossom whispered.

"I agree," Flautles said. "It is very cruel what they are doing."

They both watched through the broken pain as Catnip and Mugwort changed the labels on the bottle.

"I know. Why don't we change them back?" exclaimed Flautles.

Apple Blossom thought for a few seconds, "That's not a bad idea," she smiled.

It wasn't long before the gnome gang finished the label swapping and quietly left David's shed. Apple Blossom and Flautles waited behind the honeysuckle and, when all the gnomes had gone, they both crept into the gloomy shed and looked at the various jars and pots.

"Right! We need to write out some new labels, and put them on the correct jars," she said.

Flautles took the new labels from Apple Blossom and stuck them on the jars. Unfortunately, his eyesight wasn't too good and he put the new labels on the original jars. They both worked as quickly as they could to rectify the Gnome's quest and, after much sticking and writing, they both thought the job was done. Suddenly the shed door flung open and there stood David. Luckily, the early morning light was dim enough for David not to notice Apple Blossom and Flautles hiding under the bench. As he made his way into his shed, the two little intruders hid even further under the bench. They were very quiet as David gathered the tools he needed. He then picked up the jar of what he thought was weed spray and went on his way to the garden.

It wasn't long before David started to spray the weeds. Apple Blossom and Flautles watched from behind the clump of tall daisies. On and on David sprayed until he ran out and went to refill the sprayer with more weed spray. The weather was particularly warm and damp so it wasn't long before little seedlings started to appear. Apple Blossom and Flautles quickly sneaked over to examine the seedlings. To their horror they realised it was stinging nettle seedlings that were appearing. Apple Blossom looked across to Flautles.

"Are you sure you put the right label on the jar?" she asked. Flautles went as red as a beetroot.

"Oh I am so sorry. I must have got the labels muddled up," Flautles admitted after a little swallow.

"That's great, what a waste of time that was."
Apple Blossom said, as they quietly made their way home.

Chapter 12

THE GNOME HOUSES

Flautles and Apple Blossom approached the little row of gnome houses positioned snuggly in the hedge. The smoke was gently leaving each chimney, with the occasional spark dancing in it. The houses were almost identical, with one room downstairs for cooking and sitting and a narrow staircase leading up to a small bedroom, which had a lovely view of the garden. Luckily, as with the gnomes, each house was also invisible, so David had no idea he was being watched as he weeded the garden.

Every morning when the gnomes got up, the most important thing for them to do was check how many weeds had come up overnight. There was a large easel positioned at the side of each bedroom window with a list of various details on it, such as when a weed had been sown or planted. As each one came up it was ticked off and the list taken to Agran. He would then transfer all the information onto his very large board.

This routine had been going on for many years. In fact the gnomes had walked the same path from their homes to Agran's so often that there were little grooves in the grass where their little feet had passed millions of times. (You might have seen trails like this in your own garden, and thought it was made by animals. But now you know the real reason.)

"Thank you gentle gnomes, and of course Crabgrass and Mugwort," Agran said, as they all sat around the table in his shed.

"We seem to be doing rather well, don't you think?" Mugwort said.

"Not bad, I suppose," Agran replied, as he poured out the nettle tea. "Unfortunately, the garden people have decided to open the place to the public and have told David to get rid of all the weeds."

They all looked at each other in dismay, as this only meant one thing.

"Yes, gentle gnomes and elves. I think you realise what has to happen," Agran said, as he poured the last cup of tea.

"We must speed up the weed sowing," suggested Catnip, who sat at the end of the table. He was so small only his hat could be seen over the ridge of the table. All the others knew what he was saying as his little hat bell would ring in time with him speaking, and over the years they had all learnt bell language. That is why he is affectionately known as 'Dinger'.

"Now, that is exactly what we must do. Well done Dinger," shouted Agran, as he stood up and nearly knocked his tea over. "We will have to bring in help from the other gardens," he said.

"I could ask Fly," Ragweed shouted.

Fly had a special fan machine into which he would load all the dry light fluffy weed seeds. He would then turn the handle to make the huge wooden fan circulate and blow the seeds across the chosen patch of ground.

"We already have one, but another one of these might be useful," he added.

"And I could ask the Butterfly Squadron to help with their air bombardment," Catnip shouted.

The atmosphere was now full of excitement and everyone started to suggest what they could do. It sounded like a committee meeting.

"These are all great ideas. We must all now go out and round up some help. Then tonight we will have another meeting and discuss our next plan," said Agran.

THE BELL RINGING CONTEST

The young elves and gnomes often liked to show off their special bell ringing skills. The afternoon was warm and sunny, just perfect for the contest.

"Can you all line up please?" Flautles said.

He was always asked to judge the bell-ringing contest, so this afternoon was no different. The contestants settled back on the grass bank and rested their heads on the pillows provided. The birds settled down in the trees, and the butterflies rested their wings in anticipation of the wonderful sounds that were to come.

"I suppose you think you will win again, Dinger?" asked Flautles.

"Yes, I hope so, I think it is time I showed you how clever I am," he said, as he flicked the bell on his shoe with the end of his finger.

Crabgrass, Ragweed, Catnip and Mugwort were all lying with their backs on the grass bank, with eight little pointed shoes pointing towards the sky, each with a shiny bell attached.

"Are we ready?" Flautles asked.

Dinger answered in his normal jovial voice. "Yes, we are ready to ding."

Flautles and his musicians prepared themselves to play along with the bells, with Apple Blossom standing in front holding her Cherry Dangler (a strange accordion made of blackberry wood).

"One, Two, Three," Apple Blossom said, swaying in front of the contestants.

The delightful music drifted across the garden, accompanied by eight bells. It was always hard to judge this competition as everyone played so well, but someone had to win.

Flautles wrote the results on his score sheet and, after many minutes of thinking, he pronounced the winner. "This has been the hardest contest I have ever had to judge, but this year the winner is........"

There was the customary pause as Flautles played a drum roll on his flute (It sounded a bit silly, but there wasn't a drum available.)

"The winner of this year's Bell Ringing Contest is........"

Another pause! The Butterflies and birds fluttered their wings in frustration as it always took so long for the result to be announced.

"The winner is........"

"Get on with it!" Robin shouted, as he plucked two fleas from under his wing.

"Dinger!" shouted Flautles.

Dinger was so happy he broke into song,

I'm so happy I could fly.
See who could beat me,
Before I die."

"Oh my goodness, that is a terrible song," said Mugwort, and burst into laughter.

The afternoon soon turned into evening with much merriment ensuing. The elderflower champagne flowed and the dancing continued late into the night.

APPLE BLOSSOM TALKS TO AGRAN

"Father, I wish you could understand how much Flautles means to me, he is......"

"Stop right there!" Agran demanded. "Flautles is a useless plonker, and I don't want him to marry you, or in fact even to look at you," he shouted.

Apple Blossom slumped to the floor, her tears streaming down her little pink cheeks. She sobbed and sobbed, when suddenly Agran spoke again.

"My dear I hate to see you so upset. I will do a deal with you."

Apple Blossom looked up to her father and waited to hear what he might say.

"As you know, to be accepted in a gnome family you are expected to be fearless, honest and true."

Apple Blossom looked up at Agran dreading what he might say next, as she knew Flautles was a very timid, rather silly little Pixie.

"As you know, we are running out of the green gems from the mine. Also I must remind you if we don't get the gems, all the gnomes, pixies and fairies will lose their invisibility."

"What do you want him to do?" Apple Blossom quietly asked.

"He must enter the mine and kill the Troll."
"Ah, I think we are one step ahead of you father, as Flautles has already agreed to do just that."

Agran looked at Apple Blossom, "Are you sure?"

"Yes, he said he would do it last week."

Agran pushed his tongue even further out and said, "My word, that is amazing."

"Yes, I think he is very brave and the only way for this to work is if I go with him somehow without him knowing." Apple Blossom sighed as she held father's hand and then turned to leave.

Agran suddenly stopped her and said, "It's the only way my dear, he must prove himself."

Agran watched as his young daughter walked across the garden and disappeared into the distance. Agran sat back in his rocking chair and fell asleep, remembering when she was so young and happy.

Chapter 15

NIGHT WORK BEGINS

Everyone had gathered in Agran's shed. Crabgrass and Ragweed sat in the corner chattering about the price of paint and Catnip and Mugwort were reminiscing about the bell contest, when Agran walked in.

"Lovely to see you all here tonight, I trust you are all well?"

They all looked up from their conversations and smiled.

"We have things to discuss."

There was a nice cosy atmosphere in the shed with the soft light from the candles, and a warm glow from the crackling wood fire.

"Now I am so glad you could all come tonight," Agran said, as he stood before them with his tongue half hanging out of his mouth, just enough to sound a little less strange.

"We must make sure there is a full contingent of helpers for tomorrow night, as the humans want to display these gardens at their best and, of course, we are here to do the opposite."

The audience sat bemused, as they weren't quite sure what to do.

"Could you enlighten us as to what we are supposed to do," Young Dinger asked.

"Well, I would like you to gather as many helpers as you can from all the gardens around, and we will make sure as many weeds are planted and sown as possible tonight."

Agran then produced a large map of the garden and put it on the easel. "As you can see I have marked the spots in the garden that need to have the most attention" he smiled.

Everyone looked amazed at the amount of weeding that had to be done in such a short time.

Mugwort shouted, "Well, we had better get on with it," In his normal organised voice.

"I have made a list for all of you, so you know where and what to sow," Agran said, as he handed out slips of green paper made from dried nettle leaves.

They all looked at their leaf paper instructions and, as they started to leave, the shed door flung open.

"Good evening, gentle gnomes."

In the doorway stood an unusually tall gnome. He was slim, which was unusual for a gnome, his hat had two bells instead of one, and each shoe was adorned by an extra large bobble.

"Who are you?" asked Agran, in a very stern voice.

The very tall gnome looked down towards Agran and said, "And who might you be, you stubby little gnome?"

Agran stood as tall as he could and pushed out his chest. He lifted his chins, then stuck out his tongue, and said, "I am Agran the Chief Weed Gnome and in charge of the garden."

There was an uncanny hush in the shed as Catnip and Mugwort faced each other, as a quiet diplomatic voice could be heard from the back of the shed.

"He is very tall and handsome", Dinger said, "Could we treat him with a little respect as he is so tall?"

"What a good idea," Mugwort agreed.

"Well!" The very tall gnome said, in a confident voice, "My name is Elom the Mole Encourager."

He lifted the box he had in his hands and opened it in front of them all. They all leant over and looked into the box. To their amazement they saw a squirming mess of pink worms.

"As you see these are the worms. They will help encourage the moles to chase them and then bury their way under the lawn to then push up piles of soft soil, thus making the grass a mess of unwanted mounds of earth.

"That's so cruel, what happens to the worms?" asked Dinger.

Elom turned to him and smiled while rubbing his hands together. "I can assure you the worms won't get hurt. All I do is drop each one down a hole in the lawn. Then, as the moles approach, I pull it up and the mole pops his head out with the pile of soil."

"How on earth do you know the moles are coming?" asked Agran.

"Oh, that is simple. You can hear the scraping of their glasses against the tunnel wall," Elom said.

"What glasses?" Crabgrass shouted.

"Well, each mole is almost blind, so wears a pair of glasses to help him see. The only trouble is they are a lot wider than the mole and so, as he travels along the tunnel, the glasses make a scraping sound."

Agran stood up and lifted his hand, "I think, Elom, you have proved this is a marvellous way to slow up the garden opening, so I think he should join us."

"I agree with you sir," said Ragweed.

Soon, they all made their way to the machine shed. It wasn't long before the mice were tethered to various machines and work started. All through the night implements were whirring and clanging as the seeds and plants were distributed around the garden. Luckily the moon had shone all night and it had been an easy night's work. So, as the sun started to rise above the pine trees, the workers made their way back to the machine shed and put their tools away.

This was always the best part of the day for the Weed Team. As the sun gently rose, everyone got out their instruments and played gentle music sounding very similar to bird song. So, if in the morning you hear the birds waking up, it's probably the music played by the gnomes and elves on their way to bed.

Chapter 16

FLAUTLES TALKS TO AGRAN

Agran's daily task was to wander around the garden and watch David. He would sit, unnoticed, smiling to himself as he saw him pull up last night's weeds.

"Well that was all a bit pointless," David muttered to himself, as he pulled out numerous pink weeds.

"I just don't know where they all come from."

As he said that, there was a burst of laughter from behind the Salvia bush. David turned around and went over to where the laughter came from.

"Is anyone there?" David asked.

The only sound he could hear was a soft wind blowing through the Pampas grass. Suddenly, David noticed a figure in the mist, sitting on the mushroom. "Who are you?" David asked the apparition.

Gradually, Agran's figure appeared and he could be clearly seen.

"I don't suppose you know anything about these weeds?"

Agran looked up at David and smiled. "David, you're on a loser I'm afraid, there is no way your weeding will beat us."

David leant back on his fork and sighed. "You know, I think you are right, I can't beat you so I think I may as well go home."

David slowly put his tools neatly in the wheelbarrow, and Agran smiled. "It's not personal, but we have been weed sowing for a long time and you know what traditions are like."

David smiled, "Yes, I do, and I can understand where you are coming from."

"Oh don't try to get modern with me, you'll be talking about blue sky thinking next." Agran laughed.

"Well, I was hoping you wouldn't do you're last button up."

"What on earth are you talking about?" Agran laughed.

"I have no idea, it's been a long day," David sighed, as he pushed his heavy wheelbarrow towards the rubbish pile to dump the day's weeds.

Agran watched as the weary gardener disappeared around the corner and out of sight. Suddenly, there was a sound of music, drifting in the evening air, and it seemed to be coming from behind the large willow hedge. As Agran crept closer he could see the figure of a young pixie sitting on a stone mushroom. In his mouth there was a strange length of black wood. The young pixie was blowing gently across it and making a strange sound as his fingers moved gently across the instrument. The pixie suddenly stopped playing as Agran stood on a broken twig and made a loud cracking sound. He looked around to see Agran standing just behind him.

"That was an interesting sound," Agran said.

"Thank you," the pixie replied.

"Could I ask what it is you are playing?" Agran enquired.

"It is a Flute," the young pixie replied.

Agran stood back and listened with interest as he knew this was Flautles, the pixie that his daughter, Apple Blossom, rather liked. Agran stepped a little closer and looked deep into the young pixie's eyes. "Do you know a young fairy called Apple Blossom?" he asked with a threatening voice.

Flautles smiled and said, "Yes sir, I do. She is a wonderful little fairy and I like her very much."

"Oh, do you indeed!" Agran sneered. "I am not sure if you are quite the pixie I want to be fond of my daughter," he said, a little louder than before.

Flautles looked amazed and quietly asked, "Are you Agran the Chief Weed Gnome?"

"Yes, I am," he said, as he pulled back his shoulders and pushed out his chest. There was a sudden silence as Flautles started to put his flute away into its box.

"As much as I liked the sound of that piece of wood, it is hardly the manliest of instruments to play," Agran said, as he started to pace around Flautles with his hands behind his back.

"I would have preferred it if you played another instrument, such as the ukulele," suggested Agran.

Unbeknown to Agran and Flautles, the rest of the Weed Gnomes, and of course the Naughty Elves, had gathered close by and heard the conversation. So, when the ukulele was mentioned they all burst out laughing.

"We have heard you on that confounded thing," shouted Mugwort.

"I play the Dingbangderler," Crabgrass shouted.

"You should hear me on the Cherrydrop Medlethrop," Shouted Ragweed.

The Whistle Poddler, Trumpnose Fiddle Dump, Banglows and Stippledrops were all instruments the gnomes used for their musical evenings. The Weed Team kept mentioning various other instruments, until Agran shouted, "Shut up".

The Gnomes quickly did what they were told and immediately shut up.

"Rrrrrrr......" Came the sound from *The Wooden Thinking Man*. The Wooden Thinking Man was only a carving in a tree, but he always insisted in being involved in any confrontation that was going on. Even the statues would suggest the occasional solution if there was a problem.

Before long, there was chattering coming from the whole garden and the noise was almost deafening.

"Right, that's it!" Agran shouted.

There was suddenly silence around the garden.

"Oh, that's so much better," said the Wooden Thinking Man.

Apple Blossom looked across to where Flautles sat. He had put away his flute in its wooden box and was sitting very forlornly on the toadstool. She went over to him and put her arm on his shoulder. "Don't worry, my dear, everything will be fine. Join us as we play our instruments and you will feel much better."

"You know, you are right! A bit of music would make everything lovely again," Flautles said, as he unpacked his flute. Various other musical instruments were being unpacked ready for a good jam session. The group consisted of Apple Blossom on the Cherry Dangler, Flautles on the flute, Crabgrass on the Dingbangderler (which was a large thistle head on a string, which he hit with a twig). Ragweed was ready with his Cherrydrop Medlethrop, Catnip had his Whistle Poddler and Mugwort was on the Trumpnose Fiddle Dump. Billy Bucka held his Banglows, while Robin sang his special tune on top of the tree.

Agran sat back in amazement when he heard the wonderful music, so joined in with his ukulele. The music floated across the garden in the evening air, twisting and swerving around the bushes and trees. The birds sat silently on their branches and listened contentedly as they started to fall asleep.

As the evening came to a close, Agran went over to Apple Blossom. "My dear that was a lovely evening, and Flautles wasn't too bad either," he said begrudgingly.

"Goodnight father, thank you for staying. One day you might realise just how much of a good pixie he might make," she said, knowing what Flautles was planning to do in the mine.

Chapter 17

THE FAIRY QUEEN CEREMONY

'

Flautles looked at this year's Fairy Queen with so much pride, as Apple Blossom had been chosen. After a few minutes a small cloud drifted towards the Fairy Queen and her entourage, Crabgrass and Mugwort. They all stood in amazement as the small fluffy cloud stopped in front of them. A pair of steps appeared, leading to a comfy settee for all three. Agran stepped forward and gave his hand to assist Apple Blossom up the steps. " Let me help you, my dear," He kindly said, as she stepped on the soft steps.

Soon the cushion of soft white cloud had engulfed Apple Blossom. As she lay back, Crabgrass and Mugwort climbed up the steps and settled either side of her. Gently the cloud rose and hovered over the garden, drifting towards the lawn where everyone had gathered for the festival. There were stalls covered in fruits and other goodies from the garden, and handmade toys for the youngsters. Elom the Mole Encourager stood proudly next to his bowling game. This consisted of three holes, each with a white mouse sitting on a small mushroom in the opening. At the other end of the alley, Elom had placed a pile of acorns.

"How do you play this game?" asked Catnip, as he picked up an acorn.

"All you have to do is roll one of the acorns towards the hole and try to get it past the mouse," Elom said.

Catnip pulled back his hand and pushed the nut towards the white mouse. It rolled quickly down the alley, but it wasn't quite hard enough to knock him over, and passed the mouse to one side.

"Right, I want a go!" said Mugwort. He stepped forward and grabbed two acorns, one in each hand, and lunged them towards the frightened little mouse. Luckily, they both missed, and the mouse smiled to himself.

"Missed! You dumpy gnome" the mouse sniggered.

Mugwort went red with rage and grabbed two more nuts. He pulled back each arm and flung them towards the mice. This time they jumped to one side and let them through.

"Well done!" shouted Elom. "Here is your prize."

He brought out a huge medal with an engraving on it of a magnificent dandelion. Mugwort looked down at the medal and burst into tears, as he was so pleased. "This means so much to me. You'll never understand," Mugwort sniffed, as he brought out his hanky

.

"Why does it mean so much to you?" Elom asked.

"Well many years ago, my grandfather grew extra large dandelions and showed them at the local Weed Show.

"OOH!" Elom smiled, as he tried to touch the medallion.

"Not so fast," Mugwort said, as he pulled back the medallion. "The trouble is, while grandfather leant over a bridge looking at the fish, the medallion slipped off and disappeared into the fast running water never to be seen again. Until now!"

Many years ago, when Elom was walking along the riverbank admiring the view, he looked down and saw something shining in the mud. It was a large silver medallion. On one side was an engraving of a dandelion and on the other were the words,

'*Given for the largest dandelion.*'

He took it home and put it in a drawer until today, when he thought it might make a nice prize.

Chapter 18

THE WEED CONTEST

Early spring was always extra busy, as it was time for the annual Weed Contest. It was very important, as the weed, which won its category, would be sown in the garden the following spring.

" S'pose yours is bigger than mine," said Agran, to his old rival Mugwort, as they both wheeled their wheelbarrows onto the lawn.

"Cor blimey! Call that a dandelion head!" laughed Mugwort, as they both arrived to display their wonderful dandelion heads on the table.
A lot of care went into displaying the exhibits. Each protruding seed was carefully combed and then gently fluffed up to make it as big as possible. Soon other

contestants arrived, many with trugs, wheelbarrows and wooden boxes. Next to the dandelion head table were the couch grass exhibits, with each grass root entwined in thin copper wire, to show the judge how hard it would be to cut through it with a spade.

Then there were the Naughty Elves. They had entered the flower painting section. Luckily, they were the only entries so were bound to win. Further on next to the Gunnera plant stood a very proud gnome with Billy Bucka. Each had brought his Convolvulus exhibit. They were laid across the long table to show just how long they were. The large green leaves had all been brushed with oil to make them glisten in the sun.

" I suppose you think you'll win again this year," sneered Agran menacingly to Mugwort who stood at the end of the table.

"I might, you can never tell," he smiled back.

The garden was full of excitement now with the Nettle Weed Growers arriving. They always made the rest laugh as they both stuttered.

"DDID YYOU LLIKE MMY RRRRROOTS?" one Pixie said to the other,

"OOOH, YYES THTHEY LLOOK MMMARVELLLOUS."

The conversation between them continued with much merriment, especially when Agran started to talk with his tongue out. "Look at the size of those!" Agran shouted, as four huge builders were wheeled onto the lawn on low carts. They were the biggest anyone had ever seen, measuring the height of at least three good size gnomes. The roots were so long they dangled on the grass as the carts was paraded across to the display table. Agran was very proud of one of the exhibitors, as it was his youngest daughter, Apple Blossom.

Finally, to everyone's amusement, the pink weeds walked on. They skipped merrily across the grass and settled on the table next to the pond, their little pink flowers fluttering in the breeze.

"Well, we had better get on with the judging," Elom said, as he pulled his favourite mole onto the lawn.

"Good afternoon," Agran said with his tongue out. Elom and the mole looked at each other and sniggered.

"Do you find my Dandelion heads impressive?" Agran asked with a smile.

"Oh no, it is the way you speak that I find more impressive. Why don't you give me another few words?"

Agran smiled and then pushed his tongue out as far as he could and said, "I think you will find my speech is quite normal around here," Agran said, with his tongue hanging almost to the grass.

"Yes, I believe you are right," Elom apologetically laughed.

The pair moved around the garden slowly, continuing to make notes of the various weeds. After about an hour they disappeared, and everyone started to chatter and laugh with relief. The musicians appeared and settled under the large tree. Flautles sat close to Apple Blossom and took out his flute. Apple Blossom ran her fingers across the Cherry Dangler and all the other instruments joined them as Flautles led them in.

"One, two, three," he said as Elom and mole appeared from around the side of the Shell House and played the official ceremonial march,' Entry of the Weed Judges.'

The pair proudly marched in time to the music and stopped at the edge of the lawn.

"We have made our final judgements for this year's contest and will now read them out."

There was a sudden silence throughout the garden.

"First ….. The dandelion heads. We both felt the heads were magnificent this year, but there can only be one winner and that is Mugwort.

"Well done!" Agran, graciously said, shaking his hand.

"Now we have the couch grass contestants. It is with much pleasure we will award first prize to number two."

 A polite applause drifted over the lawn, as Elom and Mole continued to deliberate the results.

"As there was only one entry into the following category, we congratulate Catnip for his wonderful flower paintings."

He whooped with delight, and jumped around the lawn flicking paint at the unsuspecting flower heads. Billy Bucka stood very quietly as the next result was read out.

"This year's Convolvulus was the best we have ever seen, and the winner today is..........."

The silence was deafening. Billy Bucka twiddled his toes and then farted!

" ....Is Billy Bucka."

Everyone cheered and clapped, as they knew how much this award meant to him.

"Hooray!" he shouted, as he jumped up and down with excitement. The whole garden erupted with laughter and whoops of joy. Then Elom spoke again.
"Now we have the nettle growers."
Both growers stood waiting with baited breath.

"This year we would like to award the prize to both of you, as they are such wonderful examples of a good strong nettle."

Elom then swallowed a glass of nettle wine and continued.

"We were amazed at the nettles this year and give the prize to number one."

"And, finally, the pink weeds. What can you say? They are the most prolific in any garden but today they outshone the other exhibits with their softness. So, therefore this year's Weed of the Year prize is awarded to ….. The pink weeds.

At this point the music started to play everyone's favourite waltz, The Pink River. Then as the evening sun started to set, everyone settled down to a relaxing time chatting about next year's competition.

Chapter 19

THE PIXIE GOO

Flautles and Apple Blossom had picked the special goo from Jude in her little shop and took it into the garden. It was late evening and Agran with his weed team had just finished their work and gone to bed. So Flautles and Apple Blossom pulled their Goo Transporter Catapult across the grass to where Agran's work had just been done. They loaded the slings full of the magic goo, pulled back and catapulted it.

"Here we go!" Flautles said, as he and Apple Blossom released the large catapult. The goo flew across the garden to the offending growth. After a few seconds of it slithering down the weeds, they suddenly started to melt away down into the ground and disappear.

"Well, that seemed to work," Apple Blossom said, smiling at Flautles.

"Yes my dear, I think we will sort Agran and his team out now."

Flautles got out his flute and slowly pressed it to his lips. He took a large gulp of air and, with Apple Blossom playing her Cherry Dangler, they both went away happy and contented. As they neared their home, Apple Blossom put down her Cherry Dangler and started to play her Whistle Poddler that had been given to her by an admirer.

"Why are you playing that?" Flautles asked.

"I was given it by a friend," she answered.

Flautles knew the so-called friend and felt a little jealous, as any attention from another admirer was something Flautles didn't like. He was tempted to take out the whistle from the Whistle Poddler but knew Apple Blossom would be so upset. So instead, as she was putting her Cherry Dangler in its case, he quickly changed the pea inside the whistle from a round to a square one.

"There seems to be something wrong with the Whistle Poddler," Apple Blossom said to Flautles.

"Oh really my dear, what a shame."

Flautles then went very red and turned away to look at the grass. Apple Blossom looked closely into the machine, and could see a square pea.

"Oh my goodness, the pea is square," exclaimed Apple Blossom.

"My word," laughed Flautles.
Apple Blossom looked at Flautles with a very stern expression. "My dearest Flautles, as much as I love you I don't think that is very funny. Do you?"
He went even redder.

"Why are you going so red?" Apple Blossom asked.
Flautles sat down on the mushroom and put his little hands over his eyes.

"I feel so ashamed, it was me who changed the pea inside your instrument."

"Why on earth would you do that?" Apple Blossom asked.

There was a long silence, and then Flautles took away his hands and exposed two very red eyes. "I am so, so sorry, but I got so upset when I heard another pixie had given you the Whistle Poddler."

"Oh you silly little sausage, he doesn't mean a thing to me. He thinks I might like him, but honestly there is no chance I would ever return his advances."

Flautles looked deep into her eyes, and held out his little hand. "Please forgive me, I have been very unkind to you, and will not do anything like that again."

Apple Blossom squeezed his outstretched hand and looked straight in his eyes.

"My dearest Flautles, whatever silly things you do I will always forgive you, because I know you are just a silly sausage and you don't mean any harm."

Flautles pulled Apple Blossom closer to him and held her tightly in his arms. "Thank you lovely little fairy, you are so kind to me."

They held each other for so long that Flautles fell asleep on her shoulder.

"Are you snoring?" Apple Blossom laughed.

Flautles suddenly woke up. "Of course not. I was practising my nose exercises."

"Oh silly me!"

Chapter 20

FLAUTLES ENTERS THE MINE

Apple Blossom watched as Flautles prepared himself for the most terrifying ordeal he would ever experience in his short lifetime. He placed his rucksack on the table and started to fill it with things he thought he might need. First was his candle and holder with some matches and a rope, just in case of problems. He then put some elderflower tea in a flask and two elderberry sandwiches in his box. Finally he went to the cupboard and brought out a jar. Apple Blossom noticed how old the jar was, and could see a label, which read, 'only use in desperation'. How odd, she thought, as he packed it into his rucksack.

"Oh Flautles you look so sad, I wish I could come with you," Apple Blossom sighed.

"Don't worry my dear, I have to do this. It is the only way your father will accept me into the gnome family and allow me to marry you."

Apple Blossom felt a tear slowly falling down her cheek. She went over to Flautles and put her arm around his little shoulder. "I will be thinking of you all the time you are in that horrid mine,"

She gently whispered in his ear. He turned to her and looked into her sad blue eyes. "My dear, just knowing you are thinking of me will be enough to keep me safe."

Flautles pulled the heavy rucksack over his shoulder and then turned towards the door.

"Good luck!" Apple Blossom said, with a quiver in her voice. Flautles just smiled and made his way towards the mine.

It was a warm sultry night, with a full moon. There wasn't a sound to be heard as he walked through the

garden, towards the mine. Then as he approached the heavy studded door, he soon realised this was the only thing between him and uncertainty. As he put his hand out to open the mine door, there was a cry. He stopped and listened. The sound was coming from behind the door and it made him even more determined to slay the Troll.

As Flautles lifted the old rusty latch and pushed the heavy door open, there was a sudden rush of wind that blew all the dry leaves around him. Robin had been watching Flautles and flew across to Apple Blossom. She looked so sad and frightened.

"Don't worry my dear, it is time for you to be a part of me."

Apple Blossom looked up and remembered Robin's suggestion of shrinking and hiding in him.
"Remind me, what do I need to do?" Apple Blossom asked. Robin looked down at Apple Blossom and said, "If you drink some of the shrinking potion, I will hold out my wing for you to climb on, then you can climb in my ear."

She did as Robin said and then suddenly …….…
"You are a part of me now, settle down and enjoy the view."

Apple Blossom sat in amazement as she looked out of Robin's eyes. There was plenty of room inside Robin, as he had such a fat tummy. So she laid back in the warmth of Robin as he followed Flautles on his adventure.

Flautles pushed down the latch and pulled the heavy door towards him. He stood at the entrance of the mine and peered into the darkness. Then he put down his rucksack and pulled out the candle and holder. He struck a match to light up the gloom of the mine. When his eyes adjusted to the dim light, he could see figures on the ridges of the tunnel.

"Cats!" he gasped.

Each one of them looked down at him, purring with a deep threatening purr. Flautles put his hand around the candle so it wouldn't blow out and made his way past the felines, continuing further down the tunnel. As he turned the corner, in front of him floated several strange glowing shapes. They looked a lot like little moons, but shimmered in the light of Flautles' candle.

"Orbs", Robin whispered to Apple Blossom as she gazed at them slowly floating around in the darkness.
"These are said to be spirits of the departed who could never leave the mine," Robin explained.

Flautles really wished he wasn't here, and thought of Apple Blossom. As he thought of her, Flautles sensed a strange shiver going down his timid spine. Deeper and deeper into the mine Robin and Flautles went. Suddenly they all paused, as they heard music slowly drifting towards them. The sound was pleasant, but seemed to give a strange haunting message. Flautles knew about the Troll but didn't know about the music. His candle flickered and nearly went out as he pushed past a huge cobweb with a large hairy spider looking down at him. Flautles looked into the eyes of the spider, and he could see the reflection of his fear.

"What do you want?" screamed a voice.

Flautles stopped dead in his tracks and stood motionless. "I said. What do you want?"

The voice echoed around the tunnels. The sound was coming from deep in a dark cave to his left. Flautles plucked up a little bit more courage and peered into the darkness.

"I have come to ask you to release some more green gems," he said, in a very timid voice."

He stood trembling, with tears of fright dropping onto his cheeks. Unfortunately, this was what the Troll was hoping for. He knew Flautles was timid and was going to make sure he suffered. They could hear the crying of the slaves, and soon stopped in their tracks as they came to the edge of a precipice. Robin grabbed Flautles with his wing.

"Be careful!" Robin said.

"Oh Robin, thank goodness you are here. I was starting to get a little frightened."

"I think you may have started a long time ago, but let's not get picky," Robin said, as he smiled at the timid little pixie.

Apple Blossom could see what was happening and cried out to help Flautles.

"What was that cry?" Flautles asked Robin.

"Ah! That is my indigestion," Robin laughed.

"I know, why don't you jump on my shoulder, and then I could be a pirate?" Flautles said.

"Not sure if you have noticed, but I am a robin not a parrot? "Pieces of seed. Pieces of seed!"

Flautles laughed.

"I think that is enough silliness, don't you? We have serious business before us."

Flautles agreed as they both carefully crept forward.

Deep in the darkness they could see hundreds of fairy and pixie slaves digging for the green gems. There were grotesque figures, with black unkempt hair. The ugliest, cruellest faces you could imagine. The small figures had large bony feet and hands but revelled in the power they

had with their whips, lashing the backs of the unfortunate slaves. Flautles looked for a few moments and then suddenly realised he was being watched. On a beam high up in the cave was a strange creature, it had a grotesque nose and only one ear. Its body was covered in matted brown hair with hooves on its short stubby legs.

"Don't worry," said the robin, "I am here to help you."

Flautles looked up at the beam and could see the creature looking down at him.

"How can I help you?" it said.

Flautles felt a little safer now, and could feel the power of the robin creeping over him.

"So, you expect me to give you more green gems, do you?"

Flautles gulped! "Ah yes, that would be lovely," he said, rubbing his hands as if he had just washed them.

"Oh I'm sure it would be, you silly little pixie," the creature laughed.

Robin scratched his chin and thought about how to help Flautles.

"I know,"Robin said to himself, "I will summon the Orbs."

Robin quickly flew over to the swirl of glowing Orbs and asked, "Could you help us confront the Troll?"

There was an obvious realisation that the Orbs weren't too keen on the Troll either, and they slowly moved to hover over where it sat. Flautles now felt quite confident and said, "Creature, I would like you to release some more green gems straight away."

The creature looked down at Flautles and couldn't believe his cheek.

"Are you for real?" the creature laughed.

"Yes, and I have a robin to help, and if it comes to it, the orbs are with me too."

The creature sat back on its hind legs and gazed bewildered at this strange little pixie.

"Do you know who I am?" the creature asked, with a threatening tone.

"Not really," Flautles said.

"Well I am the terrible Troll who you should be terrified of, and behind you are my two pet Grindles."

Flautles looked around to see two horrible animals standing uncomfortably close.

"Well I must say you are a little tinker, aren't you?" the Troll said, as she invited her little helpers to her side.

Suddenly the atmosphere changed as the two huge Grindles moved closer to the Troll and sat either side of it. Their breath smelt like fox poo, and they tended to let out a lot of wind. In other words horrible!

"Are you impressed, or what?" the Troll said, as she pointed to her two chums.

"No, not really as I have my magic potion with me," Flautles replied.

The Troll and her two chums looked down at Flautles and smiled to each other. "Well what shall we do now?" said the ugliest Grindle. "I know!" said the other one, "Why don't we eat Flautles?" he sniggered.

The Troll smiled. "You know, that is a very good idea," it agreed.

Flautles looked up to the robin. " I think we may have a problem, Robin, as I don't really fancy being eaten?"

Robin flipped his wings and said, "I am sure we can take on these brutes and get the green gems. Oh, and also free all the slaves."

"Are you not being a little too confident, Robin?" Flautles suggested.

"I know that with you by my side, we can do anything," Robin laughed.

Unfortunately this was when things started to go wrong for Flautles and Robin. The Troll and the Grindles started to increase in size, until they were almost touching the tunnel roof, with the smell reaching a disgusting stench.

"Ah! I think we have a problem?" Robin said.
"Yes I agree," said Flautles. He then rushed to his rucksack and rummaged to find the magic bottle. He started to open the bottle.

"Oooh! What have we got now?" the Troll slowly and sneeringly asked.

"I have here my Grandfather's 'Anti Fart in a Bottle' solution," Flautles said, lifting his eyebrow.

The Grindles looked at each other, then looked a little disturbed, as their only claim to fame was their ghastly smell.

"You have now got a choice," Flautles shouted.

"Give me the green gems and free the fairy slaves or I will release my 'Anti Fart in a Bottle' solution."

The Troll looked bewildered at the Grindles and said, "It's a fair cop. I think we should do as he says."

They looked up at the Troll in amazement. "Are you sure, boss?"

"Maybe there is a way round this," Flautles asked.

"Any suggestions?" the Troll asked, as the Grindles pulled on their leashes ready to get to Robin and Flautles.

"Well, what would you want in return for letting the slaves go and releasing more green gems?" Robin asked.

Apple Blossom gazed in amazement through the eyes of Robin, and could feel the tension building up. The Troll peered down at the intrepid pair and thought for a moment. "You know there is something I would like."

Flautles and Robin's eyes opened wide with anticipation. "What might that be?" Flautles asked.

The Troll looked down at the Grindles and sighed.

"You know, we wouldn't mind a holiday. I have been stuck in this mine all my life and would like a change."

"Well I'm sure that could be arranged, I will see Agran who will sort one out for you." Robin and Flautles looked at each other and smiled with content.

"There, that wasn't so bad, was it?" Flautles laughed to Robin. "Right, we will be off now and organise a holiday for you."

As Robin and Flautles turned towards the mine entrance and were about to leave, there was a shout.

"Excuse me, where do you think you are going?"

Robin and Flautles stopped and turned back towards the Troll. "What's the problem?" asked Robin.

"You can't just leave, there has to be the mandatory fight, with a few injuries and maybe a death or two." The Troll laughed. "How do you think Agran would ever think you are a proper pixie if we didn't have a fight so that you could prove your braveness?"

Flautles looked bemused at the Troll. He thought for a while and whispered into Robin's ear. "What do you think, Robin?"

"I don't think we have much choice if you want to marry Apple Blossom."

Through the eyes of Robin, Apple Blossom could see and hear what was happening, she so wanted Flautles to be brave, but was scared he would get hurt and cried out to Flautles. "Be careful my darling!" Flautles looked at Robin. "Did you say something?" Robin blushed and said, "No, nothing to do with me," As he stepped back and twiddled his claws.

"Hmmm!" Flautles thought, as he was sure he heard something.

"Well what is it to be?" the Troll asked in a teacher-like manner.

"I suppose we will have to have a fight," Flautles said with a deep sigh. "How do you suppose we should start this affray?"

The Grindles raised one side of each of their mouths and showed their green manky teeth.

"I know how we would start," said the ugliest Grindle.

"Oh calm down, let's do it in a fair fashion," the Troll suggested. "If you put your fists up and look fierce, I will unleash the Grindles."

Flautles didn't at first, as he was now rather frightened. Robin stepped forward and then they raised their fists and feet. "OK we're ready, give us what you've got."

At this point the Troll smiled, and leaned over to unclip the Grindles' leashes. Within a few seconds they were on top of Robin and had knocked Flautles to one side. Robin wasn't very strong and couldn't put up much of a fight. He fell back and could feel life leaving him. Robin lay on his back with his feet pointing towards the cave roof. Apple Blossom also lay on her back inside Robin and looked out of his eye. "Please help!" she quietly cried.

Flautles picked himself up and crawled towards the cry for help. He could hear a sound but didn't know where it was coming from. The Grindles came slowly towards

Flautles. He squinted and looked into the eye of one of the Grindles. There seemed to be a reflection in it. As he looked closer, there in the reflection was Apple Blossom. Flautles couldn't believe what he was seeing. He peered even closer to be sure.

"Excuse me, what do you think you are doing?" the ugliest Grindle asked.

"The thing is, I am sure I can see Apple Blossom in your eye."

"Oh don't be silly, that is my sty," the Grindle said.

"No I am sure I can see Apple Blossom in the reflection in your retina."

"Oh for goodness sake, have a closer look why don't you?"

Flautles leaned over and lifted the Grindle's eyelid. There he could see a distinct image of Apple Blossom. Flautles turned towards Robin who was lying very still on his back. He went closer and then bent down. As he peered into his eye there was Apple Blossom. She was just a faint haze, but he knew that it was her. "Please get me out," a delicate voice asked.

Flautles stood in amazement and then he remembered the bottle of magic potion he had in his rucksack. Robin lay motionless and Flautles just had to do something to bring him back to life to save Apple Blossom. He opened the flap of his little brown rucksack and brought out the small bottle. He prised open the cork, and a sweet smell of roses floated into the air. Flautles leaned over Robin and released two drops of the magic solution over his head. Nothing happened for a moment until suddenly there was movement of one of his wings. Slowly the wing started to move a little more, followed by the other one. Soon Robin seemed to start breathing and slowly sat up.

"Thank goodness, you seem to be recovering," Flautles said.

Inside Robin, Apple Blossom could feel the warmth coming back into his little chubby body. She didn't like the cold and felt a nice glow as Robin started to breath properly again.

"Can you help me now?" Apple Blossom cried.

This time Flautles saw her face as she cried to him. He looked at Robin and asked, "What can I do to let Apple Blossom out?"

Robin smiled to Flautles, "If you think of your best wish and look into Apple Blossom's eyes while holding my wing, she will slowly be released. Slowly a sheet of mist seemed to engulf Robin and slowly Apple Blossom was rising from within him. She gently glided down next to Flautles and caught his little cold hand.

"Ah, at last, thank you. I so wanted to be with you my little dear," Apple Blossom said, as she squeezed Flautles' hand.

"Is that enough of a fight?" Apple Blossom asked the Troll who had patiently watched it all going on. The Troll looked down at them and smiled with a proper Troll smile. "Yes, it is the only fair way out of this problem."

Suddenly the Troll lifted her claw and pointed to the waiting slaves. "Come on my dears, it is time for you all to leave."

The slaves looked in amazement and started to scramble out of the tunnel to freedom.

"Aren't you forgetting something?" Flautles demanded. "What about the green gems?"

Reluctantly, the Troll pushed forward a truckload of freshly dug gems. "Here you are, take the lot, and I hope you will be happy with them.

"I will now see Agran, and ask him to organise your holiday," Flautles said with a very confident air. "Oh, by the way, do you have a preference for your holiday destination?"

The Grindles looked up at the Troll and said, "How about Norway? Yep that sounds good, I have a few relatives over there."

"Right, I will organise that if we can now have the slaves."

The Troll smiled and summoned the slaves to be released. Flautles looked in amazement as hundreds of tired slaves came out of the darkness and ran to safety out of the tunnel.

Flautles, Robin and Apple Blossom felt very proud as all three pushed the truck of gems out of the mine.

FLAUTLES HAS A PROBLEM

"What is the matter Flautles?" Apple Blossom asked. She could see he wasn't his normal shy self, but very fidgety. Flautles looked towards the slim little fairy that stood in front of him with the moonlight bathing in her soft golden hair. The reflection on the waterfall made Flautles quiver as he came even closer to her.

"My dearest Apple Blossom, I have a confession to make," he said, looking down at the bells on his shoe.

Apple Blossom's heart stopped. "What have you done now, you silly sausage?"

"Oh no, it's nothing I've done, but what I want to do."

She looked bemused as the little pixie stood before her. Flautles looked so timid and afraid. Apple Blossom went closer and put her soft gentle hand on his cheek.

"Don't be afraid my dear little angel, I am here for you,"

Flautles smiled, and put his hand into her warm grasp. He closed his grip on her and pulled both of their hands down in front of him. "I want to ask you something, my dear," he said squeezing her hand.

"Maybe a little less squeezing would be nice," Apple Blossom suggested.

"So sorry my dear," he laughed, but then continued. "Now that I have been into the mine and hopefully proved myself to your father, would you consider..."

He stopped and looked away. There was a tear in his eye. Apple Blossom took out her hanky and gently wiped away the small teardrop sliding down his cheek.

"Why are you so sad?" she whispered.

"Oh I'm not sad but frightened, as I have to ask you something very important."

Apple Blossom looked and smiled, the gentlest smile he had ever seen. "Please ask me what you want to say," she said.

Flautles gulped. "Would you consider marrying me?"

There was a sudden silence as the owl and all the other animals waited to see what Apple Blossom's answer would be.

"My dear Flautles, yes of course I will.'

Suddenly the garden erupted with cheering and applause. The birds chirped, Mr Owl hooted, Crabgrass and Ragweed got out their instruments and joined Billy Bucka for an impromptu concert. Everyone was so happy that Agran heard all the noise from his workshop.

As with all fairyland traditions, stones are given to each other. Apple Blossom had thought Flautles might have asked this question tonight and had come prepared. In her pocket she had a little white stone with one word on it. "Fab." Flautles looked at the pebble and smiled, "What does that mean?"

"When our initials are joined together it spells 'Fab'. So, you see, everything will turn out fabulous!"

Flautles put his arm around her shoulder and held her even closer. He had also prepared for this occasion, and held out a flat slate. Apple Blossom looked down at the slate and saw there was a painting on it.

"That looks lovely, what is it?" she asked.

"Why don't you look closer?" Flautles said, as he held out the slate closer to her. She turned away, as she realized what it was. "It is our rock by the waterfall," Apple Blossom said, with a croak in her voice.

"Yes my dear, this is where we sit in the evenings and listen to the water."

"Oh you are a silly old romantic fool," she said, as she fell into his warm embrace. They both looked at each stone and then into each other's eyes. There was nothing else to say.

Chapter 22

THE WEDDING

At last they were to be together. After many years of anguish they were now to be married. As with all pixie and fairy weddings there were no rings, but a simple medallion. This coin was given to the bride's father who took it to the silversmith. He would cut it in half and place both parts in presentation boxes made of woven willow. At the ceremony they would be presented to both partners as a sign of long lasting love, by the sacred wise old owl. Another peculiarity for a pixie wedding was the choice of 'best pixie'. He was always chosen from a selection of pixies looking the least like a weed.

"Are we all ready?" asked Robin, as he looked down from his favourite tree.

"Yes, we are ready and waiting," Mugwort shouted.

The 'best pixie' candidates lined up on the edge of the lawn. Each one dressed to look like his favourite plant. Crabgrass stood proudly in blue as he was supposed to be a bluebell. He was splendid in his blue cap and matching tunic and held his blue bell. Ragweed stood next to him, adorned in red, trying to be a rose. His shoes matched the splendid hat he wore with drooping petals. Then there was Catnip. Being so small, he disguised himself as a daisy. He wore a hat and yellow scarf, which didn't match the orange waistcoat and trousers. The bells on his shoes shone brighter than a dollar. Finally, there was Mugwort dressed just like a tulip.

"Well it's up to you," Robin said, as Flautles gazed at the four candidates. "You know, I think I will choose the one in red," he said.

Ragweed stepped forward and shook Flautles' hand twice, skipped around once, and then bowed. Another tradition.

"At last, we are ready for the wedding," Robin happily said.

It was a warm sunny afternoon. The birds were sitting on their favourite branches for the best view. All the bunnies and white mice sat under the willow tree, while the pheasant family assembled next to the waterfall. All the guests sat on the toadstools facing towards Agran's memorial stone. It was very unusual for a human to be invited to a gnome, fairy or pixie wedding, but there, in the middle of it all, very proudly sat David the gardener and Jude the fairy godmother. They were delighted to have been invited, as they both knew what an honour this was.

"Have you booked the cloud?" Agran asked the 'best pixie.'

"Of course I have," Mugwort said confidently. Luckily he knew the cloud owner and could rely on it turning up on time.

The musicians started to play the magical pixie wedding music. As each note floated into the afternoon air, the leaves floated gently to the ground and danced amongst the waiting guests. Butterflies drifted slowly across the waterfall among the blue and white dragonflies. The gnome, elves, pixie and fairy guests waited in anticipation as the music came to its climax.

"Are you ready, my dear?" Agran asked Apple Blossom.

They both stood at the back of the gathering, as Apple Blossom's bridesmaids adjusted her white daisy chain dress. The music suddenly stopped and the guests turned towards the most beautiful wedding they had ever seen. As they slowly walked towards Agran's stone, the sound of butterfly wings could be heard gently fluttering. The robins sang an especially composed song for the day and in the pond could be heard the deep hum of the hidden frogs.

"We are gathered here to celebrate the marriage of Apple Blossom and Flautles. Could you all give them a rousing cheer?"

Everyone stood up and cheered with delight as the happy couple knelt at the stone.

"Do you have the medallions?" the wise old owl asked. Mugwort stepped forward with the ceremonial cushion that held the two halves of the medallion.

"As a sign of eternal commitment, I would like to present you both with these two halves," the owl said as he held Flautles little shaking hand.

"Flautles, I would like you to take this chain and put it over Apple Blossom's neck." Flautles lifted the long sliver chain and slowly placed the half medallion over her neck. He then stepped back as the old owl said,

"Apple Blossom, could you now place the other half over Flautles' neck?" She picked up the long slender chain and placed it around Flautles' thin neck. As she did, she leaned forward and gave him a gentle kiss on his forehead.

"It is now my pleasure to announce that Apple Blossom and Flautles are married." the wise owl announced.

The whole garden seemed to erupt with joyous laughter and music as the happy couple walked towards the waiting cloud. The large white, fluffy cloud floated patiently above the grass as Apple Blossom and Flautles climbed the fluffy steps.

"Good luck my dears,"

Agran shouted as the cloud ascended in to the evening air and floated towards their honeymoon destination.

"Does anyone know where they are going for their honeymoon?" Billy Bucka asked.

"I was told they are going to Norway! They will pick blackberries and bring them back for us to make a huge pie!"

Printed in Poland
by Amazon Fulfillment
Poland Sp. z o.o., Wrocław

51392064R10088